ABCers

by **Carole Lexa Schaefer**

illustrated by **Pierr Morgan**

VIKING

An Imprint of Penguin Group (USA) Inc.

A is for arm linkers.

B is for Book readers.

C is for Color drawers.

D is for Dog walkers.

E is for Eek! squealers.

F is for Friend greeters.

G is for Giggle givers.

H is for Hot dog eaters.

I is for Ice cream lickers.

J is for Jump takers.

K is for Kitten petters.

L is for Lap sitters.

M is for Monkey climbers.

N is for Noise makers.

O is for Owie getters.

P is for Piggyback riders.

Q is for Question askers.

R is for Race runners.

S is for Song singers.

T is for Tiptoe dancers.

U is for Umbrella sharers.

V is for Veggie growers.

W is for Water splashers.

X is for Xylophone plinkers.

Y is for Yawn stretchers.

Z is for Zzz snoozers . . .

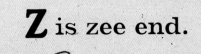

VIKING
Published by Penguin Group
Penguin Young Readers Group, 345 Hudson Street, New York, New York 10014, U.S.A.
Penguin Group (Canada), 90 Eglinton Avenue East, Suite 700, Toronto, Ontario, Canada M4P 2Y3
(a division of Pearson Penguin Canada Inc.)
Penguin Books Ltd, 80 Strand, London WC2R 0RL, England
Penguin Ireland, 25 St Stephen's Green, Dublin 2, Ireland (a division of Penguin Books Ltd)
Penguin Group (Australia), 250 Camberwell Road, Camberwell, Victoria 3124, Australia
(a division of Pearson Australia Group Pty Ltd)
Penguin Books India Pvt Ltd, 11 Community Centre, Panchsheel Park, New Delhi – 110 017, India
Penguin Group (NZ), 67 Apollo Drive, Rosedale, Auckland 0632, New Zealand
(a division of Pearson New Zealand Ltd.)
Penguin Books (South Africa) (Pty) Ltd, 24 Sturdee Avenue, Rosebank, Johannesburg 2196, South Africa

Penguin Books Ltd, Registered Offices: 80 Strand, London WC2R 0RL, England

First published in 2012 by Viking, a division of Penguin Young Readers Group

5 7 9 10 8 6 4

Text copyright © Carole Lexa Schaefer, 2012
Illustrations copyright © Pierr Morgan, 2012
All rights reserved

LIBRARY OF CONGRESS CATALOGING-IN-PUBLICATION DATA IS AVAILABLE
ISBN: 978-0-670-01231-2
Special Markets ISBN 978-0-670-01537-5 Not for Resale
Manufactured in China · Set in Barbera · Book design by Nancy Brennan

This Imagination Library edition is published by Penguin Young Readers, a division
of Penguin Random House, exclusively for Dolly Parton's Imagination Library,
a not-for-profit program designed to inspire a love of reading and learning, sponsored
in part by The Dollywood Foundation. Penguin's trade editions of this work are
available wherever books are sold.

To my extended family of sisters and brothers—

Mary,

Dave and Marianne,

Sylvia and Roland,

Flora and Ray,

Judy and Jim,

Doug—

arm linkers all. —C.L.S.

x x x

To the ABCer girls, Anika and Sabrina,

and most especially to my son Aaron and his Special K, Kelsi. —P.M.